# CATS DON'T DANCE

# CATS DON'T DANCE ™

A novelization by Francine Hughes
from the screenplay by
Cliff Ruby & Elena Lesser and Scott Alexander & Larry Karaszewski

## SCHOLASTIC INC.

New York   Toronto   London   Auckland   Sydney

ISBN 0-590-30844-0

12 11 10 9 8 7 6 5 4 3 2 1                      7 8 9/9 0 1/0

Printed in the U.S.A.        40
First Scholastic printing, March 1997

# 1

A time in the past . . .
In the big city of Hollywood. . . .

A breeze blew through a grand pink mansion.
The wind ruffled pink frilly curtains. It swept over
a heart-shaped couch. A heart-shaped chair. A
heart-shaped table.

In one bedroom, a spoiled little girl tossed and
turned. She was Darla Dimple. Child movie star.
She had big blond curls tied with pink ribbons.
And even in her sleep, she wore a great big pout.

*Zzzzz*, Darla snored loudly. A servant named
Max tiptoed into the room.

Max had huge legs, huge arms, and a very tiny
head. He towered over the heart-shaped chair. He
loomed over the heart-shaped couch.

Carefully, Max set down a pink breakfast tray.

He poured "Darla Dimple" cereal into a heart-shaped bowl. He straightened his white gloves.

As usual, Max woke Darla. Then he handed her the newspaper. Darla's picture was on the front page. Darla grinned. Nothing pleased her more.

"Look, Max!" she cried. "I won another award. It's from the ARF Foundation. And it's for sweetness. Generosity. The gift of love and laughter to animals around the world!"

At the award ceremony later, the announcer smiled at Darla. He said she was kind to animals. He called her "Hollywood's biggest little star. America's sweetheart."

"Hey, Miss Dimple," a reporter called. "How about a picture with some animals?"

"Why, sure," Darla said in a sweet voice. "I'm the luckiest little girl in Hollywood!"


While in the small town of Kokomo, Indiana . . .


A crisp breeze blew through the streets. The sun shone brightly. It was a terrific day.

A young cat named Danny stood at the bus stop. He *felt* terrific. He felt like he could do anything.

Danny's green eyes flashed. His golden fur glowed. He fixed his green vest. He tipped his straw hat. His animal friends crowded close to say good-bye.

Big crocodile tears rolled down the crocodile's cheek. "We'll miss you," he called. "So long!"

"Good luck, Danny," the horse said. He handed Danny a horseshoe. A sheep gave Danny a wool sweater. And twin calves gave Danny a banner that said "Hollywood."

Hollywood, movie capital of the world! Danny couldn't wait to get on the bus and be there.

Danny was crazy about movies. He loved them all.

But most of all, Danny loved musicals. Big musicals. With songs and dances, and lots of flashy numbers.

Danny wanted to be a star. To sing and dance and act. Danny knew he had talent. He thought that was all it took. He thought anyone could make it in the movies.

Even an animal.

# 2

Day turned into night. Then night turned into day. The bus to Hollywood bounced through cities and towns. Past farms and forests.

Finally the bus arrived.

Hollywood, Danny thought excitedly. He watched the sun rise over a hill. I'm finally here. Hollywood Boulevard!

In a wink, Danny jumped off the bus. He stashed his clothes and gifts and banner on the sidewalk. He wanted to see the sights. The people. The stars.

The street was empty.

Danny shrugged. What else would you expect? It was only sunrise.

One small penguin pedaled by. He rode a tricycle with an igloo on the back.

The penguin braked. He hopped off the tricycle.

Then he tried to unload a block of ice from his igloo. He pushed. He pulled. But the ice didn't budge.

Danny leaped to help. They carried the ice together. Danny grinned. It felt so good to leap! He did it again. And again. Danny couldn't help it. He had to leap and dance.

"I got on a bus," he sang out "and came to the town where dreams come true. It will happen for me. It can happen for you."

The penguin blinked. "For me?"

Danny nodded. He kicked up his heels. He jumped onto a park bench. Then he flipped onto the next bench . . . and the one after that. He shuffled. He spun. His paws went *tap, tap, tap.*

Hollywood Boulevard filled with people. Horns honked. Tires screeched.

Danny spotted a taxi. He waved good-bye to the penguin. Quickly he jumped inside. A pretty cat was running for the same taxi. But Danny didn't notice. The taxi zoomed off. And it left a cloud of dust behind.

"Oh!" exclaimed the pretty cat, covered with dirt.

Danny poked his head out of the taxi roof. He waved his banner at the big Hollywood sign in the hills. He gaped at movie stars. He stared at famous sights.

A few minutes later, the taxi pulled up to an office building. Danny flipped the driver some coins. Then he jumped outside.

A big fountain stood outside of the building. Danny danced around it. He spun, arms out wide. His banner waved in the wind.

Danny closed his eyes and circled wildly. The same pretty cat walked by.

"Uh-oh," she said, spying Danny. She tried to skitter past. *Whomp!* The banner whirled around her tightly. Danny jerked his arm. The banner untwisted. And the cat reeled — *splash!* — into the fountain.

The cat sat up, dripping wet. She glared at Danny. Her big brown eyes snapped.

"Hollywood!" Danny shouted, not seeing a thing. He scooted into the building and up to the fifth floor. Then he paused outside a door. The sign read: FARLEY WINK: ANIMAL ACTORS AGENCY.

Danny grinned. This was the place.

# 3

Inside the agency, animals packed the waiting room. A hippo, a fish, a goat, and a turtle crowded around the watercooler.

A giant bear lumbered out of Farley's office. The bear frowned. He looked down at his script.

"Bear rug lies on the floor," he muttered. He dropped the page. "I knew I'd be a walk-on. But *I'll* be the one who is walked on here."

Frances the fish flipped her long scarf. She struck a glamorous pose. "Hmm!" she said with a laugh. "A star is born!"

Cranston, the grumpy old goat, sat down on the couch. He and Frances were dance partners. And they always agreed. "What did you expect?" he asked the bear. "You're an animal."

The sweet-faced hippo was named Tillie. She

wanted the bear to feel better. "At least it's a part," she told him.

The bear shot her a look.

"Okay, not a great part," Tillie continued.

Silently, the bear stared.

"Okay, okay, not even a good part. But it's work."

Tillie paused a moment, then added. "All right. So it's not a lot of work. And the pay is lousy. But . . . but . . ." Tillie trailed off. She couldn't think of one nice thing to say.

T.W., a nervous turtle, clutched a good luck charm. He pulled a fortune cookie out of his shell. "It says, 'give it up, you loser,'" he read out loud.

"Oh, now," said Tillie. "Our luck could change. Soon . . . I think . . . I hope."

Danny suddenly burst into the room. "Well, hi there!" he cried. "How you all doing? Mind if I sit down?"

Danny bent to sit on the couch. But Cranston scooted over.

"Excuse me," Danny said, almost landing on Cranston's horns.

"Don't mind him," Tillie told Danny. She stuck out her hip, bumping Cranston across the room. "He was just leaving."

She turned to Danny and giggled. "I'm Tillie." Then she introduced the others.

"I just got into town," Danny explained. He pulled out a list. He looked it over carefully. "Now let's see," he said. "Go to Hollywood." He checked off the line. "Check."

"This is my plan. Right here," he told the others. "I have it all figured out. I'm going to work real hard. And I'll have a big part by Friday."

Cranston snorted. "Right."

"Oh, sure," said Frances.

Tillie straightened Danny's vest. "They're casting a big Noah's Ark movie," she told him. "You know, with a boat and a giant flood? Lots of parts for animals." She glanced at the secretary's desk. It was empty. "Sawyer's not here yet. So you go into Farley's office. Let him know you're here."

Danny smiled. "Thanks, Tillie." He peeked inside the other room.

Papers covered Farley's desk. Six telephones were ringing — all at once.

"Listen you big ape," Farley shouted into one phone. "I need those two monkeys now!"

Farley picked up the next phone. "Little Timmy is in tears?" he cried. "So what? I want that collie!"

"Get off the line," he yelled into the third phone. "I'm casting the boat picture. *L'il Ark Angel*."

Danny knocked. "Mr. Wink?"

"Yes?" said Farley.

"If ya have any openings for a talented cat, I'm your man. Uh, cat."

But Farley had been talking on the phone. "Yes, let's see," he continued.

Farley looked over his file. "I have two burros. Two camels. Two caribou." He tapped the paper. "Cats. I need cats."

Farley lowered the list. He noticed Danny, standing in the doorway.

"Say, you," he asked. "Can you play a cat?"

"I am a cat!" Danny told him.

Farley chuckled. "How would you like to be in a Darla Dimple movie?"

Danny's eyes opened wide. "*The* Darla Dimple? America's sweetheart? Lover of children and animals?"

"One and the same," said Farley. He waved a bunch of papers in Danny's face. "Just sign here and here and here and here."

In the waiting room, the door swung open. The pretty cat hurried inside. Water from her hat dripped onto the carpet. A puddle formed at her feet.

"Sawyer!" said Tillie. "What happened?"

"Did you walk under a ladder?" T.W. asked. "Smash a mirror?"

Cranston eyed her wrinkled dress. "Have you *looked* in a mirror?"

"A cat crossed my path," Sawyer fumed.

Tillie glanced into Farley's office. "Orange tabby?"

"Yeah." Sawyer nodded.

"Green vest? Straw hat?"

"Yeah, yeah. How did you know?"

Tillie beamed. "Hippo intuition." She brushed Sawyer's hair. She smoothed out her dress. "You want to look pretty," Tillie told her. "You might meet someone nice."

Sawyer laughed. "Right."

Who would she ever meet typing and filing? She picked up an armload of papers. Then she trudged over to the file cabinet by Farley's door. "He's going to waltz through that —"

The door suddenly opened. *Smack!* It hit Sawyer, pushing her against the wall. Hiding her from view.

Farley nudged Danny into the room. He eyed the empty desk. "Where's Sawyer?" he asked.

The door creaked open. And there was Sawyer, picking up papers.

Farley grinned. "Sawyer! Sweetie! Baby! I can't find a female cat for the ark movie. Guess who's going to fill in?"

Sawyer shook her head. "Tough tabby. I'm a secretary. Not an actress."

"I'll pay you double," Farley begged.

Sawyer looked him in the eye. "Triple."

"Triple?" Farley threw up his hands. "Okay, okay. Triple." He pushed Danny closer. "Here's your partner."

Sawyer gasped. It was that cat! "Forget it," she snapped. But she knew she had to do it. A deal was a deal.

Danny gazed at Sawyer. He took in her pretty brown eyes. Her cute little nose. Even when she scowled, she seemed sweet. Danny sighed.

Already, he was falling in love.

# 4

**D**anny and Sawyer stood outside Mammoth Studios. Danny grinned. This was the place. The place where movies were made. And Danny was about to step inside — right into his first role!

The two cats walked through giant gray gates. Danny gazed at the elephant head carved on top. Then he blinked. Shining Mammoth Tower rose before him. Danny gazed around, wide-eyed.

"Excuse me," someone said, hurrying past.

The lot bustled with people. Actors. Directors. People pushing cameras. Pulling racks of costumes.

Danny and Sawyer passed a big ape. He was smashing little toy cars.

"Hey, Kong!" Sawyer called. "How is the picture coming?"

"Oh!" the ape sighed. "Don't get me started!"

Sawyer led Danny to Sound Stage 13. Inside, a fat little penguin trailed behind a donut cart.

"Go away," the donut man told him. "These are for Miss Dimple." He gave the penguin a shove.

"Okay," the penguin said. He turned to leave. *Bang!* He bumped into Danny. Dozens of donuts rolled out of his shirt.

The penguin blushed. "I'm busted," he said.

Danny helped the penguin to his feet. Then he recognized him. It was the penguin from Hollywood Boulevard.

"Hey!" Danny patted his shoulder. "What are you doing here?"

"That ice thing is just a side job." The penguin held out a flipper. Danny shook it. "Name is Peabo Pudgemyer," he told Danny. "But you can call me Pudge."

*B-r-i-n-g* rang a bell. "Oh!" Pudge exclaimed. "It's time to start!"

Danny hurried to wardrobe. When he came out, he wore a blue sailor suit. Danny peered around. Ducks, horses, lions. All the animals wore sailor suits.

A whistle sounded. The animals lined up two by two. They marched to the stage. A bright pink ark bobbed on cardboard waves.

"Script! Script!" a young man called. He handed

a bunch of pages to Danny. Quickly, Danny thumbed through them.

His heart beat fast. Where were his lines? There!

Cat #1: Meow.

Danny scanned the script again. Where were his other lines?

"Meow?" Danny said, confused. "Where's the rest?"

Sawyer sighed. "That's all there is."

"But this is a musical!" Danny protested. "We're supposed to sing and dance."

"This town has rules," Sawyer explained. "Around here cats say meow."

"But that's so old hat." Danny grinned. "I'll jazz it up a little. I'm sure no one will mind."

Sawyer flung up her paws. He just wasn't listening. "All right," she said. "Learn it the hard way."

"Meow, meow," Danny practiced. He purred softly. He purred loudly. He purred with an accent.

Sawyer looked at him, worried. What would happen? What would the director think?

Just then Flanigan, the director, strolled onto the set. He yelled into a megaphone, "Quiet!"

Everyone fell silent.

"Miss Dimple is ready to begin," Flanigan announced. "Lights!" Giant lights clicked on.

"Camera!" The camera whirred.

"Action!" Flanigan cried. "Cue the elephant."

Woolie the elephant appeared in every Mammoth movie — trumpeting before the movie began.

Now he stepped into place. An assistant rushed over. He plopped a hairpiece on Woolie's head. Then he stuck tusks on each side of his trunk.

Woolie trumpeted. The filming had begun!

# 5

A chorus sang softly. A beam of light floated down from the sky. Darla drifted down with the light, swinging by wires. She wore fluffy angel wings. A halo shimmered above her head.

Darla hovered above the ark. The animals pranced below her.

Darla sang about the boat. About saving the animals.

"The cow went . . ."

"Moo!" said Cow #1.

Darla went on to piggies, and birdies, and doggies. And then she sang, "The kitty-cat went —"

"Meow!" purred Sawyer.

"Meeeeeow!" Danny sang out. He leaped in the air. "Meow, meow, meow. Talking 'bout the boat. Meow, meow. On the sea. Meow, meow."

Danny slid across the stage on his knees. He

came to a stop, arms held out wide. The music trailed off. Danny looked up.

Everyone stared at him. And no one looked happy.

"Meow?" he squeaked.

"Cut!" Darla shrieked from above.

"Oh, yes!" Flanigan agreed hastily. "Cut!"

"Who's the star here?" Darla demanded. "Let me down this instant!"

All the assistants rushed to help. They hurried to a big lever. In a panic, they pulled hard. Darla shot down to the ground. *Bump bump!* She hit the stage.

Darla's face turned red. She kicked her chubby legs.

"Sweetheart," Flanigan said, hurrying over. "Darling. Angel."

"That's right," Darla screeched. "I am an angel." Her voice rose even louder. "An adorable little ANGEL!"

Dozens of people scurried over. They brought chocolates. Hot fudge sundaes. Toys. Games. "Your ducky?" one assistant offered.

Darla slapped the toy away.

"I hate animals!" she shouted. She pointed to Danny. "Especially that one!"

Surprised, Danny stepped back. "Oops!" he said, falling over the lever.

The lever shifted. *Whoosh!* Darla flew into the air. She swung left. She swung right. She was swinging out of control!

Once again, everyone rushed to help.

"Max!" Darla yelled.

Everyone stopped in their tracks.

*Boom! Boom! Boom!* Footsteps sounded through the set. Tillie cowered behind a skinny crane. T.W. leaped into a crocodile's mouth.

*Crash!* Max smashed through a wall. He stomped across the floor. *SQUEAK!* He flattened Darla's ducky with one huge foot.

Max lifted his arm. He caught Darla in the middle of a swing. Then he set her gently on the ground.

Again, Darla pointed at Danny.

"Yes, Miss Dimple," Max said. He reached down. He wrapped one big hand around Danny.

"Nice knowing you," whispered Cranston.

Max lifted Danny into the air and asked him, "How does the kitty cat go?"

Danny gulped. "Meow?"

"Very good," Max said, and opened his hand. *Thud!* Danny fell to the ground.

Flanigan clapped his hands. "Okay, everybody! From the top!"

# 6

The day was over. Filming had ended. The animals left the set. "Meow, meow. Boop boop de boop," they sang out. They were all making fun of Danny. Even Tillie slid on her knees, pretending to dance just like him.

Danny stood a few feet away. Hurt, he shook his head. He began to shuffle away.

"Danny, wait!" Tillie cried, feeling bad. Sawyer sighed. "I'll talk to him," she told the others. "Somebody should set that cat straight."

Sawyer strode over to Danny. He was looking over his list. "Let's see," he murmured. "This could set me back a whole day." He paused and thought a bit. "Nah. Maybe only half a day."

He turned to Sawyer. "I don't get it. What happened in there? Did I hit a sour note?"

Sawyer started to speak. "Well —"

"'Cause if I hit a sour note," Danny continued, "I could go back. I could fix it. I could. I mean —"

"Danny!" Sawyer interrupted. "They don't care. Don't you get it?"

"But I just want to sing and dance," Danny insisted. "I want to do the things I love. Doesn't everybody?"

Sawyer shook her head. How could she make him understand? People looked down on animals in Hollywood. "I - I - it's not that simple," she stammered.

"It is in Kokomo," Danny said.

"Then . . ." Sawyer spoke slowly. "Maybe you should have stayed there."

# 7

Danny slumped against the stage door. He needed to think. To figure things out.

"Is this why I came to Hollywood?" he asked himself. "To say meow?"

Pudge stepped up to Danny. He waved his flipper in the air. "I was going to slug that big dumb Max," he told Danny. "But I didn't want to hurt him."

Danny smiled weakly.

"And what about that Dimple kid?" Pudge continued in a tough voice. "What's her problem? I thought you were great."

Danny straighted up a bit. He gave Pudge a real smile.

Pudge kicked up his heels. He tried to do the steps Danny had done. But it was hard with webbed feet. "Whoa!" he cried, falling with a thud.

"I'll show you," Danny offered. He got to his feet and tapped his toe. A piano struck a note. Danny tapped both feet. More notes tinkled. Danny twisted and turned. Pudge followed him step by step. They speeded up the moves. And the music sped up, too.

Pudge had it. He was dancing!

Suddenly Danny froze. He'd just realized there was music. "Where is it coming from?" he asked.

Danny and Pudge followed the sound to an old circus trailer. The two friends climbed a tree. Then they peered through the window.

Inside, an elephant played the piano. Danny scratched his head. Those eyes. That face. He knew this elephant. He looked back at the elephant head on Mammoth Tower.

"It's him!" he whispered. "The Mammoth mascot. Woolie!"

Woolie stretched his trunk to hit a note. The music swelled. Danny slapped his knee to the beat.

Woolie held his feet above the keys. There was one final note. What would it be? Danny held his breath, waiting.

Suddenly Woolie spun around on the stool. Danny and Pudge jumped back. The tree bent with them. Snap! The tree jerked forward. Danny and Pudge hurtled into the air . . . through the window . . . into the trailer.

Danny sprawled on the rug. Pudge landed on a piano key.

"B flat!" Woolie exclaimed. "The perfect note." He patted Pudge. "You have a rear for music, little fellow!"

Then Woolie noticed Danny. "Say," Woolie said, helping him up. "You're the fellow from today. The one who made all that trouble."

Danny blushed. "I really upset Miss Dimple."

Woolie gazed back, serious. "Yes, you did." Then he broke out in a smile. "Jolly good show!"

Huh? Danny thought. Why is that good? Before he could ask, a teakettle whistled.

"Ah!" Woolie said. "Care for a cup? It's a special peanut brew!"

Danny and Pudge nodded. Smiling, Woolie lumbered into the kitchen area. *C-r-e-a-k!* The whole trailer tilted with his weight. Danny and Pudge skidded across the floor. Plop! They tumbled onto the couch.

Woolie took a few steps to the right. *Creak, creak, creak.* The trailer tipped right. Three cups flew out of the cabinet. Woolie caught them neatly.

Then Woolie took a few steps left. *Creak, creak, creak.* The trailer tipped left. Three peanuts dropped out of another cabinet. Plop! They fell into the cups.

The trailer lurched and swayed as Woolie finished the tea. Danny and Pudge held each other tight.

At last Woolie finished. He brought over the tea and sat down. The trailer stopped rocking. Danny sighed with relief.

"Oh!" Woolie suddenly exclaimed. "Would you like some cream?" He leaned forward, about to get up.

"No! No!" Danny and Pudge cried at the same time.

Danny sipped his tea. Then he turned to Woolie, eager to ask about the music. "Did you write that song for a movie?"

Woolie laughed. "No," he answered. "I wanted to write music for the movies. But what do they want?" He waved a foot at his hairpiece and tusks. "They want me to be a mascot."

"What a waste," Danny said.

"It's the same for everyone." Woolie pointed his trunk at some photographs.

Danny saw Tillie singing. Cranston and Frances dancing. T.W. dressed for a pirate role. Danny sucked in his breath. A pretty cat smiled in the last photo. She wore a long, sparkly gown and held a microphone.

"Is that Sawyer?" Danny asked.

Woolie nodded. "I really thought she'd make it. Such a dancer. Such a singer!"

Danny couldn't believe it. Sawyer had hopes? Dreams? The cat who told him to forget his?

"But the spotlight will never shine on animals," Woolie went on. "That is the way it will always be."

Danny listened to Woolie. But he was thinking. Thinking of a way to change it.

"Unless . . ." Danny murmured. "We remind the animals."

"Of what?" asked Woolie.

"Why they came here to begin with," Danny replied.

# 8

The next day hundreds of animals waited by the studio gates. The alley was hopping. Rabbits. Kangaroos. They were all there, hoping for work.

A studio assistant gazed at the crowd. "All right," he shouted. "This movie is a jungle stampede. I only need water buffalo. The rest of you can go."

A loud sigh rose up. Slowly, the animals padded and scuttled and flew away.

T.W. turned to go. "Well," he told his friends. "Might as well go home and clean."

The turtle disappeared inside his shell. *Vroom!* He switched on a vacuum cleaner.

All at once, Danny leaped out from behind some boxes. He pulled Pudge along beside him. "Hey, everybody!" he shouted.

T.W. poked out his head. Cranston blinked.

"Well, look who's back," the goat said in a bored voice. He nudged Frances to keep moving.

"Hey, everybody!" Danny shouted again. "Don't let this old town get you down!"

Before anyone could leave, Danny jumped into a Dumpster. He pawed through old props and costumes. Then he tossed out a cape for Frances. A pirate hat for T.W. A scarf for Tillie.

Pudge waddled up to another garbage can. He found forks and knives and empty cans. Homemade instruments! *Dum, dum, dum.* Pudge beat a can like a drum.

Danny danced to the beat. Cranston crossed his hooves. Frances yawned.

But Danny wasn't finished yet. He flung open a studio door. Woolie sat inside, playing a piano. Music filled the air.

Danny grabbed a mop. He plucked the strings like a banjo. The whole street rocked with the tune. Tillie clapped. Cranston shrugged. Then he grabbed Frances for a tango.

In her office, Sawyer heard music. The *tap tap tap* of paws and hooves. She typed a letter. *Click, click, click* went the keys.

Were those animals? Sawyer wondered. Dancing? Singing?

Sawyer stopped typing. She squinted out the window. They *were* animals!

Danny wants to be a big star. He leaves his
life on the farm to go to Hollywood!

In Hollywood, Danny heads straight to an animal actors
agency. "Do you need a cat with talent?" Danny asks
enthusiastically. "I'm your man. Uh, cat."

Danny gets the part. He's going to the magnificent
Mammoth Studios. He will be in a movie with the famous
child actress, America's sweetheart, Darla Dimple.

But Darla Dimple is not as sweet as she looks. One of the
first things she says, or screams, is, "I hate animals!"
Then she points to Danny. "Especially *that* one!"

Suddenly Danny hears footsteps. *Boom! Boom! Boom!* It's Darla Dimple's bodyguard, Max. Danny is in trouble now. . . .

Danny shows the other animals that he really is talented. That he really can sing and dance.

Darla invites Danny for tea at her huge pink mansion.

Unfortunately she serves animal crackers.
It makes Danny think of his friends.

Danny and the animals set up a special performance
for the president of Mammoth Studios. But things
don't go as planned. . . .

In fact, it's a disaster!

Could Darla Dimple have anything to do with it?

Danny and Pudge come up with a new plan. They
will impress the head of Mammoth Studios on the
night of Darla Dimple's movie premiere.

Darla Dimple arrives at the movie and the crowd goes wild.

After the movie is over, the animals want to perform
on stage. Max, the bodyguard, has another idea.

The animals finally make it to the stage. They give a great performance.

And that's just what Danny and his friends did. They changed Hollywood forever — and became stars.

She leaned out the fire escape for a better look. *Creak!* The ladder slid down, taking Sawyer with it. Sawyer bounced off, right between Cranston and Frances.

Danny shuffled over. "Hey, Sawyer! Dance with me?"

"This is a waste of time," Sawyer told him. "You'll never dance in the movies."

Sawyer glanced at her office window. There were letters to be typed. Work to be done. She headed out of the crowd.

But Tillie bumped her. Sawyer tripped past Danny. He held out his paw and caught her as she dipped to the ground. They were dancing!

"Come on," the animals cheered.

Sawyer hesitated. Then she did a simple tap dance.

"Not bad!" Danny scooted up the fire-escape ladder. "A little rusty. But hey? Who's perfect?"

"Rusty?" Sawyer snorted. She twirled up to the ladder. One more spin, and she kicked it hard. Danny tumbled into the Dumpster.

Sawyer grinned. She shuffled her paws. She leaped and whirled. She still had it. She could still dance!

Danny leaped out of the dumpster. He joined her. Step for step, they matched each other's moves. It was like they'd been partners for years.

The others gathered around. They clapped and whistled.

Finally Danny flung Sawyer out in a spin. He pulled her back. For a long moment, they gazed at each other. Then they broke away, embarrassed.

"Like I said," Sawyer told Danny as she walked back to work. "Dancing is a waste of time."

Then Danny spied a poster on the wall. A picture of L.B. Mammoth, head of Mammoth Studios.

"What if I got you an audition?" Danny said suddenly. "A tryout with L.B. Mammoth?"

Sawyer stopped in her tracks. She wanted to believe Danny could do it. She really did. But she knew it was impossible. She shrugged and kept going.

The others nodded sadly. Sawyer was right. Why even bother dancing and singing? One by one, they left the alley. Only one remained. Pudge. He tugged on Danny's shirt.

"Can you really do it?" he asked. "Get us an audition with the boss?"

Danny smiled. "It's worth a try!"

The two friends walked away. They didn't see Darla step into the alley. They didn't know she'd been listening all along.

And Darla had a plan of her own.

# 9

**D**anny stood outside Darla's door. "Calm down," he told himself. "Just calm down."

Danny couldn't help but feel nervous. Darla Dimple, America's sweetheart, asked to see him! She invited him to tea. This must be something big, he thought.

He gathered his courage. And he knocked.

Max let him in. Darla sat at a little, heart-shaped table. Daintily, she reached into a bowl. She held out one pinky, and picked out an animal cracker.

*Snap!* She broke it in two.

Darla smiled sweetly. "Thank you for coming, Donald."

"Uh . . . it's Danny," Danny said.

Darla giggled. She offered him a cookie.

Animal crackers? Danny shook his head.

"No?" Darla said. "Well, more for me." She stuffed the head in her mouth.

Danny gulped.

"I wanted to apologize for Max," Darla went on. "The other day on the set? Oh, he was bad!"

Darla bit off another head. "He was terrible."

She chewed on cookie after cookie. "Awful." *Chomp, chomp, chomp.* "Horrible."

"I want to make it up to you," Darla told Danny.

Max slapped a big piece of cake on the table.

Danny cleared his throat. "You don't have to do anything."

"Oh, I insist," Darla said. "Is there anything you need?"

Danny peered around the cake. "No."

Darla blinked. "Isn't there someone you want to meet?" Her voice grew louder. "The head of the studio, maybe?"

Danny looked at her.

"I could introduce you!" Darla shouted.

"Oh!" Danny smiled. "Could you help me and my friends? We'd like to perform for L.B. Mammoth."

"Oh, Dennis," Darla said softly. "I'd be delighted." She picked out a cookie. "Why," she said, as if she'd just had a thought. "Maybe you can all do a number in my movie."

Danny leaned forward. "You mean it?"

"It's just what the picture needs!" Darla told him. "You can use the set. The ark. Anything you need. Just get the animals ready. Friday, three P.M. I'll make sure L.B. sees it."

L.B. had a press conference Friday at 3 P.M. Reporters, photographers would all be there. Darla knew L.B would show them the set. And it all fit perfectly with her plan.

Darla snapped the head off a cat cookie. Danny was so excited, he scooped up the rest. He munched right along with Darla.

Then Darla dropped her voice. "Please keep this quiet, Dino. I don't like people to know about my good deeds."

# 10

It was Friday afternoon, almost 3 P.M. Animals scurried around the Ark set. Pudge sat way up high in a control booth. He flipped a switch. Thunder boomed. He pressed a button. Lightning crackled overhead.

"Thunder and lightning. Check!" Pudge announced into a microphone. "Special effects all ready."

Danny waved from the stage. "All right everybody!" he shouted. "Mr. Mammoth will be here any minute. Get into position. Do what you did in the alley."

Danny gazed at all the hopeful faces. So much depended on this. "And remember," he added. "Don't be nervous!"

T.W. shook in his shell. "N-n-n-nervous? Why

would we be nervous?" For luck, he reached for a rabbit's foot.

"Hey!" cried the rabbit. "Leave my foot alone!"

The stage door opened. The animals swung around. Was it L.B. already? Was he early?

Sawyer poked her head inside. Everyone went back to what they were doing. Glancing around, Sawyer took it all in. Animals setting up instruments. Practicing songs. Getting into costume. She strolled over to Tillie and Frances. They were getting made up.

"Well, well, well," Sawyer said. "Run of the set. Use of the ark. Costumes. Something smells fishy."

"Fishy?" Frances huffed. "I beg your pardon," she said.

"Sorry," Sawyer apologized. "But I smell a rat."

"Excuse me?" a rat sniffed.

"Oh, never mind," Sawyer said.

Just then Danny hurried over. "So you're joining us?" he asked Sawyer.

"No." Sawyer shook her head. "It will never work. Besides, how did you get all this stuff?"

Danny grinned. "Oh," he told Sawyer. "A little angel is looking out for us."

Danny chuckled. Then he turned serious. "Come on, Sawyer. Your life isn't in that office."

He held out a sparkly costume. He closed Sawyer's paws around it. "Dance with me," he begged. And then he left, not waiting for an answer.

"Well?" Tillie said. She powdered Sawyer's nose.

"I can't do this," Sawyer told her.

Tillie dabbed her again. "So?"

"I can't do this," Sawyer repeated.

Tillie helped her into her costume.

"I can't believe I'm doing this," Sawyer said, all ready to go on.

Danny stood at the helm of the ark. "Pudge! Start the rain," he shouted. "When L.B. shows, we'll sing and dance."

T.W. scuttled by. He gripped a fortune tightly. "Abandon ship!" he read with a groan. "Rough waters ahead!"

# 11

In the control booth, Pudge reached for a switch. But two shadowy figures stepped in front of him. One big, one small.

Max and Darla.

Darla snapped a long coil of rope. And she edged closer.

In another part of the studio, reporters and photographers gathered for the press conference. A giant Darla Dimple billboard loomed on stage. Flanigan stepped in front of it.

"Ladies and gentlemen of the press," he announced. "I bring you the founder of Mammoth Pictures. L.B. Mammoth!"

The crowd *oohed* and *ahhed*. L.B. strode on stage in a fancy suit. He grinned at the audience. Flashbulbs popped. Reporters called his name.

One reporter pushed his way to the front. "Mr.

Mammoth!" he called out. "What's the secret of your success?"

L.B. held up a hand. The crowd fell silent. "Simple," he told them. "It's Dimple!"

L.B. pointed to the billboard. The audience went wild. L.B. grinned, as he described the child star. "Perky . . . adorable . . . innocent . . . sweet . . ."

At that exact moment, Darla smiled sweetly at Pudge. Then she tied him up.

"Sorry, penguin," Darla said in a soft voice. "But into each life, some rain must fall."

"Max!" she shrieked. "Man the valve!"

"Yes, Miss Dimple." Max gripped a wheel at the front of a ceiling pipe. He gave it a twist. Water sprinkled down.

The rain looked perfect. Danny gave a thumbs-up sign.

"More water, Max!" Darla screamed. "We need more water!"

Max pushed against the pipe. He heaved with all his weight. The pipe cracked, then cracked some more. Water gushed out in a flood.

"Wind, Max!" Darla called. "We must have wind!"

Max ripped the cover off a giant fan. He spun the blades. Great gusts of air blew through the set.

Danny looked at the water lapping against the

boat. He shielded his face from the wind. This was too much storm! What was going on?

The water rose. Higher. Higher. It lifted the ark off the ground. Waves slapped the deck. The boat tossed and turned. Animals gripped the railing. They skidded from side to side. Danny felt the giant boat move forward. He gripped the steering wheel tight.

"Thunder!" demanded Darla. "Lightning!"

Max bent two power poles close together. He rubbed them hard. Sparks flew. Lightning lit the ceiling. Then Max gave the valve one more twist. The pipe burst with a boom. Thunder!

A tidal wave of water rushed out. It carried the ark up, up, up . . . then down, down, down. Sawyer raced to join Danny. They tried to pull the steering wheel. They tried to push it. But the boat swept along, out of control.

Up in the control booth, Darla laughed. Any minute now, L.B. would bring reporters onto the set. He'd see the mess. Blame the animals.

Darla and Max climbed a ladder to the roof. They escaped into bright sunshine.

And left the animals to their fate.

# 12

L.B. stood by the stage door. Flanigan hovered close by. Reporters crowded around, eager to see the set.

L.B. opened the door with a grand wave of his hand.

Everyone gasped. A wall of water towered above them. *Whoosh!* It dropped. Water spread everywhere. It was like the ocean — a rough and stormy ocean. And it carried everyone in its wake.

The ark careened this way and that. Animals shouted. They squeezed into life jackets.

"Throw the anchor!" Danny ordered.

Tillie flung the anchor overboard. *Rrrip!* It snagged on something. L.B.'s jacket — with L.B. in it!

"Save me!" Flanigan groaned, holding fast to L.B.

The ark rushed forward, pulling the anchor . . . and L.B. . . . and Flanigan.

L.B. shot out of the water. He skipped along the surface like a water-skier.

"Oh, no!" cried Flanigan, riding on his shoulders.

The ark lurched into set after set. Roaring waves crashed through scenery. People screamed and fled.

Cranston hung his head over the side of the boat. "It doesn't get worse than this," he wailed.

Then his horns wrapped around a flagpole.

"Whoah," Cranston cried as he flipped over. Over and over he went. Finally he landed on Flanigan's shoulders.

"Goat overboard!" Tillie shouted. The boat tipped suddenly. "Goat — *oomph.*" Tillie soared into the air. She dropped onto Cranston's shoulders.

Tillie gazed down at Flanigan, and below him L.B. "How awkward!" she giggled. "I don't believe we've met."

The ark picked up speed. It whirled around a corner. "Watch out!" Danny cried. *Crash!* It plowed into Mammoth Tower.

L.B. and the others skied into the building. They swept past his secretaries. "Morning, Mr. Mammoth," they said one by one as the foursome shot by.

The ark blasted out the other side. But all that pounding . . . it was too much. The boat stopped moving. It listed to one side.

It was sinking!

L.B., Flanigan, Tillie, and Cranston stopped, too. For a moment, they hung above the ship. Suddenly they plummeted. The anchor swung. The rope wound around the mast. Around and around. It pinned L.B. and the others to the pole.

The ark sank lower.

"Abandon ship!" Danny shouted. "Abandon ship!"

The animals jumped out. They bobbed to the surface in their life jackets. Danny floated around. He made sure everyone was okay.

The ark foundered. The mast dipped into water. Lower and lower.

L.B., on the bottom, glared at Danny. The water rose to his shoulders.

"You animals will never —" The water covered his mouth.

"Nibble kibble in this town again!" Flanigan finished.

# 13

L.B. ordered the animals to leave. He told them never to come back. Ever.

Guards herded everyone outside the gates. The animals were wet and tired. But most of all they were disappointed.

Their dreams of singing and dancing in the movies? Dashed — along with the ark. And now, they wouldn't get *any* work. Not even a *woof* or a *baa*.

Danny stood under the Mammoth arch. He tried to explain to the people inside.

"The animals!" he cried. "It wasn't —"

The gates clanged shut in his face.

"— their fault," he finished quietly.

Danny's eyes fell on his friends. Shivering. Unhappy. What happened? he wondered. What went wrong?

*Screech!* A fancy pink car braked right by Danny. Darla stuck her head out the back window. "Nice working with you." She laughed.

Max tossed Pudge out the door. The penguin blinked. He coughed up water. Then he smiled at Danny.

Darla shook her head in disgust. "Singing and dancing animals? Ha!"

The car squealed away. The crowd turned to Danny, staring.

"*She* was your angel?" Sawyer said.

"She said she wanted to help us," Danny explained.

Tillie's eyes widened in surprise. "And you believed her?"

"Darling!" Frances said. "She was acting. She hates animals."

"Always did, always will," Cranston added in a glum voice. "Sawyer was right. You should have stayed in Kokomo."

Sawyer caught her breath. When someone else said it, it sounded so mean.

Woolie sighed. "Go home, son," he said sadly. Then he lumbered away.

"Wait, wait!" Danny pleaded, Pudge at his side.

But one after the other, the animals left.

Only Sawyer hung back. She heard Pudge ask, "So what will we do now?"

And she heard Danny answer, "Nothing. I'm on the next bus out of here."

# 14

The animals gathered at a nearby diner. They drank coffee. And they complained about Danny.

"This is all his fault," T.W. started.

"I never trusted him," added Frances.

"Nothing but trouble," muttered Cranston.

"I have to admit it," Tillie said. "We were better off before."

Sawyer sat alone at the counter. She listened quietly. But suddenly she had had enough. She stood and faced her friends.

"Okay!" she said. "So Danny messed up!"

Everyone stopped talking.

"But at least he tried," Sawyer continued. "He believed in something. And so did you."

Sawyer gazed down at her paws. "I did, too."

Shaking her head, Sawyer left the diner. A second later, Tillie ran after her. "You know," Tillie said, smiling, "you can still catch him at the bus stop."

Sawyer smiled back. Tillie was right. She could catch Danny. Convince him to stay. In a flash, she raced down the street. Her paws thudded on the sidewalk. Faster and faster. She had to get to the bus stop in time.

Sawyer rounded a corner. She spied the bus stop . . . and the bus just pulling away. She cried out, "Wait!" But it was too late. The bus kept going.

Then she saw Danny's hat, still on the bench.

At least I'll have something to remember him by, she thought.

Sawyer picked up the hat. Danny's list was tucked into the brim. A tear rolled down Sawyer's cheek.

Would she ever see him again?

# 15

Danny gazed out the bus window. He had to get his last look at Hollywood. He had to see everything one more time.

The bus passed Pudge and his ice tricycle. Mammoth Studios. Famous stars. The Hollywood sign. Everything Danny had seen on his first day there.

But Danny noticed other things now, too. Hungry animals, waiting in line for food. Animals without homes, huddled in front of fires. Danny slumped in his seat.

"Poor fools," the driver muttered. "Trying to be something they're not. Animals belong on farms. Not in movies."

Danny straightened. He knew the driver was wrong. Animals could be anything they wanted to be. Anything at all.

Suddenly Danny spotted a poster for *Li'l Ark Angel*. "Stop the bus!" he cried.

He had another idea.

Quickly Danny found Pudge. He explained his idea. Pudge nodded, excited. And they hurried into action.

First the friends snuck into Mammoth Studios. Then they crept into an office. Danny opened cabinet after cabinet. Finally he found the *Li'l Ark Angel* file.

Here it is! he thought. He flipped through some papers. The invitation list!

Lots of famous people were being invited to the movie opening. Danny grinned. He had some names to add.

Across town, Tillie peered into her mailbox. An invitation? she thought. To where? Cranston and Frances, T.W., Woolie, and Sawyer each received an invitation, too.

Curious, Sawyer ripped open her envelope. She was invited to a movie opening! She grinned happily. It had to be Danny.

# 16

It was the big night. The opening of *Li'l Ark Angel*. People lined the street by the theater.

Movie star after movie star paraded inside. Everyone clapped and cheered. Suddenly the crowd went wild. "Darla!" they shouted. "It's Darla Dimple!"

Darla waved sweetly to her fans. She posed for photographers. She smiled one last time, then slipped through the door.

A few minutes later, Frances, Cranston, Sawyer, Tillie, and Woolie walked up to the theater. Nobody clapped. Nobody cheered. They all wondered what animals were doing there at all.

Inside the theater, Sawyer spotted five empty seats. Sawyer sighed. She didn't want people to notice them. But these seats were in the middle of a row.

As quietly as possible, the animals slid past the people. Woolie sat down. The other seats shot up. "Oomf!" went the people as they bounced up high.

At last the lights dimmed. The movie began. Darla's face filled the screen. In the audience, the real Darla grinned. Max handed her a drink. Darla took a dainty sip.

Then she burped.

Everyone watched the movie. No one noticed Danny and Pudge creep through a side door. Quietly they stood backstage, behind the giant screen.

Pudge brushed off his feathers. He'd gotten dressed up for the big event. He straightened his brand new bow tie.

"Now," Danny whispered. "The minute the movie ends? We're on!"

Pudge nodded. He yanked his tie. *Snap! Snap!*

In the audience, Max heard the noise. His ears perked up. Then he tiptoed away.

Meanwhile, Danny set up the lights. Pudge rolled a drum into the center of the stage. Oops! He bumped into a wall.

Wall? Pudge thought. What wall?

The little penguin gazed up — right at Max.

With one swipe of his hand, Max lifted Pudge. He rubbed Pudge's feathers to make static. Then he stuck Pudge to the ceiling.

"Pssst! Danny!" Pudge hissed. "Look behind you!"

Danny turned. Max! He ran around ropes, with Max chasing behind. He raced behind backdrops. Finally he climbed a walkway that led to the roof.

Danny clamored outside. He was high above the city streets.

But so was Max.

Danny heard the big man thud closer. And closer. Danny edged to the side. *Thud. Thud. Thud.* Danny shuffled a little further.

"Aahhh!" He fell off the roof.

Max grinned and rubbed his hands. His job was done. He turned to leave. But he caught sight of the Darla balloon. It rose before him — with Danny sitting on top.

Quickly Max grabbed the balloon rope. He scrambled up and faced Danny. Then he lunged.

Danny batted his paws. He tried to pounce. But he was no match for Max. He slipped and slid . . . away from Max . . . back, back, back. Close by the roof.

The roof! Danny thought. It has a point — a spire!

Danny skidded some more. He tumbled off the balloon. Onto the roof. Max started to follow. But Danny grabbed the rope. He tugged the balloon . . . over to the spire.

Max gasped.

Danny tugged again. The point pricked the balloon. *Pop! Whoomph!*

"Ahhhh!" cried Max as the balloon sputtered away.

Danny watched Max grow smaller and smaller. He heard his cries grow fainter and fainter.

And then there was silence.

# 17

The movie was ending. Danny didn't have much time. Quickly he climbed into the theater. He grabbed Pudge from the ceiling and they scurried backstage.

This is it, Danny thought. The only chance I have left. He took a deep breath. Then he burst onto the stage.

"Ladies and gentlemen," he announced. "Please wait!"

All eyes turned to Danny. Darla's jaw dropped in surprise. The animals stared. He's here! Sawyer thought happily. He's still here!

"Tonight we honor Miss Darla Dimple," Danny continued.

A few people clapped. But most looked confused. "This cat," they whispered. "What is he doing?"

"And because Darla Dimple cares," Danny went on, "she's arranged a special treat for you."

Darla began to protest. But Danny raised his voice. "It's a live show!"

The audience cheered.

"With an all-animal cast!"

The cheering stopped.

Frances, T.W., and Cranston grumbled. They wanted no part of this . . . no matter what it was. They got up to leave.

"An all-animal cast?" Danny repeated. "Unheard of! But Darla is America's sweetheart. Lover of children and animals."

Again, Darla tried to speak up.

Danny hushed her. "Come on, Darla. Take the credit. You asked us to perform. Now where are my friends?"

Danny gazed into the audience. He saw five empty seats, and his heart dropped. They'd left. And he was all alone.

Danny stepped back, not sure what to do. The audience murmured. Darla laughed. "Silly cat!" she said. The crowd laughed with her.

The whole thing was falling apart.

Should I stay? Danny wondered. Or should I slink away? Go back home — for real this time?

Suddenly he felt someone take his hand. Sawyer! She stood beside him, smiling.

"We're all behind you," she whispered. "Got them?" she asked Tillie.

"Got them!" Tillie said, backstage.

Danny turned. Tillie held Cranston, Frances, and T.W. in a big hippo hug.

The animals struggled. Danny sighed. They didn't want to be there, Danny knew.

"Look," Danny told them. "If you like how they think of you, then you can go. I almost did."

He paused then added quietly, "But you'll never forget that feeling. The feeling when you dance," he said to Frances and Cranston.

"When you play the piano," he said to Woolie.

"When you sing," he said to Sawyer.

The animals stopped struggling. They grinned and nodded. Danny was right. They could never forget that feeling.

"Come on!" Danny shouted. "Let's show them!"

# 18

**D**anny jumped in front of the curtain. "Hit it, Pudge!" he cried.

Pudge let loose, playing the saxophone. The others sang and danced. They acted out their hopes. Their dreams.

The audience leaped to its feet, clapping.

Darla raced backstage. *She* was the star. She, Darla Dimple. And she had to stop these animals right now.

Darla flipped a switch. The spotlight turned on Danny and Sawyer.

The audience clapped harder.

Darla pressed a button. A long, thick rope dropped down. Quickly, Darla hooked T.W. up to the end. The turtle swung out over the seats. He swung back, landing on stage with a smile.

The audience cheered.

Darla turned red. She hit switch after switch. She pressed button after button.

Fireworks rained down. The stage lit up bright and beautiful. A Statue of Liberty rolled out.

The audience whistled and *oohed* and *aahed* and cheered even more.

Darla stamped her feet. She tossed her curls. Then she saw the biggest switch of all. She lunged for it, pulling hard.

A trapdoor opened beneath her. *Whoosh!* Darla fell through. She tumbled down a chute. "Oh!" she cried, slipping and sliding. Finally, she somersaulted onto stage.

Darla stumbled to her feet, facing the animals. "I'm the star!" she screamed. She glared at Danny. "You stupid cat! I should have drowned you when I flooded the stage."

"Oops!" Darla clapped a hand over her mouth. Slowly, she turned to the audience. The crowd looked back, shocked. Everyone heard. Everyone knew Darla Dimple had wrecked the Ark set. Not the animals. But America's sweetheart.

Pudge pulled a lever. The trapdoor slid open again. "NOoooooo," Darla cried, plummeting down.

The crowd jumped up and down, shouting "Hooray! Hooray!"

The animals laughed and took a bow. Then

Sawyer pulled Danny off to the side. She showed him his old, crumpled list.

"Let's see," she said, looking it over. "Land a big part? Check. Get the girl? Check."

Sawyer leaned over, about to kiss Danny. But before she could, Flanigan rushed over.

"Sweethearts!" he gushed. "Darlings!"

"Get a picture!" L.B. ordered, coming up behind him. "These kids are making history."

And that's just what Danny and his friends did. From that moment on, animals starred in musicals. In westerns. In dramas and comedies.

They changed Hollywood forever. Thanks to one cat — his hopes and his dreams.